Adam loved his new home.

It was high, high in a tall tower in the city.

It was exciting. He was living in the sky.

THE SEEDS OF FRIENDSHIP

MICHAEL FOREMAN

WALKER BOOKS
AND SUBSIDIARIES
LONDON · BOSTON · SYDNEY · AUCKLAND

But Adam missed

the faraway place

where he used to

live. Every evening

he asked his mum

and dad to read him

stories that brought

back memories of

their old home.

Adam drew pictures

to go with the stories

and pinned them on

his bedroom wall.

But when he looked from

his bedroom window, he

saw a very different picture.

He saw a cold, grey world.

It seemed so empty, too.

Sometimes he saw children

playing far below in the shadows of the buildings,

but he was too shy to go down and say "hello".

Then one morning Adam couldn't see
out of his window at all. The glass
was frosted over and the icy patterns
reminded Adam of a frozen forest.

With his finger, Adam drew animals to
live there.

When his window-forest was full he
ran to the next window, and the next,
and the next, until every one was full.

That night Adam saw

snow for the first time.

In the morning, the dark, grey world was gone.

It was a white wonderland! Adam rushed

downstairs and out into the snow. It was so cold!

Some children were

building a snowman.

Adam touched the snow. It was light and wet and cold
all at once. He started to build a snow elephant.

"That's a bit small for an elephant!" one of the
children laughed. "Let's make a big one."
Then they threw a snowball at him.
Adam laughed.

So they all worked together to build

the biggest elephant that they could.

When they had finished, Adam started to make a snow hippo

and then a snow crocodile. The other children copied him

and soon there were snowy

rhinos, lions and a camel, too.

By supper time, the

snowman was in charge

of a whole snow-zoo!

A few days later, when the snowy world had melted, it
was time for Adam to start at his new school.

He was pleased to see that some of his new friends
were there. They showed him around. Adam's favourite
place was a small garden. It was a wonderful splash
of green in the grey playground.

Adam's teacher gave him some seeds from the garden to take home. He gave them to his mum. He didn't know what kind of seeds they were, but Mum planted them in the window boxes.

"Let's see what happens," she said.

As the months passed, the school's garden grew and Adam brought more plants and seeds home. Once the window boxes were full, Adam and his friends found tin cans and pots and pans and carried them up to the roof. Together they made a garden in the sky.

"Let's make more gardens!" said the children.

So Adam and his friends made gardens on

any patch of waste ground they could find.

Now, Adam no longer sees a grey world.

He sees a city of gardens.

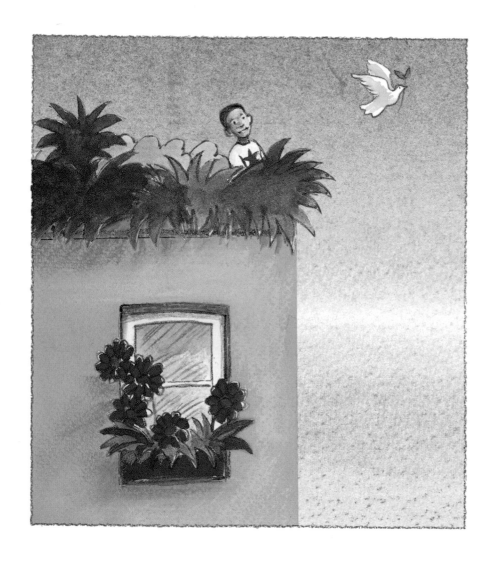

He knows that each season will bring

its own wonders and colours, and that

the seeds of friendship will never die.